GRIFFEN THE MOUNTAIN MAN

SUITOR'S CROSSING: THE CALDWELLS #5

HALLIE BENNETT

I0619503

Searching for more from Suitor's Crossing?

Check out the Mountain Men of Suitor's Crossing series <u>here</u>[1]!

CHAPTER ONE

GRIFFEN CALDWELL

Caldwell Sunday dinners are sacred.

Everyone congregates around the dining table for good food, the latest news, and plenty of sibling teasing, which is why it's usually my favorite part of the week.

Except lately things have been changing.

"Hey, Griff, can you pass the potatoes?" Kennedy asks from her place across the dining table, and I absentmindedly hold the ceramic bowl out to her. My sister brought the first change when she fell in love with her military pen pal.

Then, our brothers, Ezra and Soren, met their *heart sparks*.

And now, even our commitment-phobe brother has settled down.

It's not that I begrudge my siblings their happiness, but with each new addition to our family tradition, I'm reminded of what I don't have.

A partner in life.

I haven't even had a girlfriend since a disastrous prom night over a decade ago.

Instead of women and dating, my life revolves around caring for our grandpa. A choice I don't regret, but it was easier to accept back when my brothers and sister were also single and focused on the responsibilities of their everyday lives.

Stabbing my knife into the garlic chicken on my plate, I cut another piece free and try to shake off the unsettling feeling of upheaval that's been my constant companion the last few months.

More and more, my mind has been drifting into pity party territory. Like the older I get, and the less I have to show for my age, the more depressed my thoughts become.

It's fucking annoying.

Wanting more but not knowing how to get it.

Not knowing exactly what kind of *more* I'm searching for.

Gramps clears his throat at the head of the table. "I've got an announcement to make..." His gaze slides over each of us, pausing on me for a second longer, and my gut tightens in anticipation. "There's no easy way to say this, but I'm moving into Golden Living to be with Greta."

Silence hangs in the air before Kennedy jumps from her seat to hug Gramps. "Congratulations! I'm so happy for you guys."

A round of happy encouragement rises from my siblings while I remain quiet. Not an unusual state of being for me, but this time it's more than just being a man of few words.

Gramps and I have lived together for years. Despite his independent nature, I've been his caretaker, and he's been my best friend. But with this news, my role will soon change, and I'm not sure how I feel about that.

Who are you kidding?

You're fucking terrified.

"Griffen, are you okay?" Diana, Soren's girlfriend, nudges my elbow, concern written in her expression at my reticence.

I'm not unhappy about Gramps's news. He and Greta are cute together. She's brought a spark back into his life, especially since our grandma died over a decade ago.

But as selfish as it sounds, I wish he hadn't decided to move into the town's senior living community.

Wish he wasn't choosing to leave me behind.

"I'm fine." What else can I say? Begrudging my grandfather's happiness would make me an asshole. Addressing the table as a whole, I force myself to ask, "When are you moving?"

What's the timeline before my life implodes?

"Well, we ain't getting any younger," Gramps jokes, and everybody laughs. Even I grin at his usual good humor. "I figured we'd start packing my belongings immediately, and once that's done, pick a day we're all free to move into Golden Living. Ideally, before the holidays get into full swing in November."

Damn, that's quick.

The calendar might have just flipped to October, but it's my life that got flipped upside down.

CHAPTER TWO

HEIDI WAGNER

So, this is how I go.

Not by old age or freak accident, but by a fucking blue and white gingham ribbon that will be the death of me.

"No matter how many ways I maneuver the fabric, the edges keep flipping," I growl in frustration, untying the damn thing for the fourth time to start again.

"It doesn't have to be perfect, dear," Greta says from a floral-covered sofa where she's filling out the form for her entry into the Picnic Basket Auction.

"I don't need perfect," I mutter, "I'd settle for pretty, or not looking like it's been mangled to death." My fingers loop the ribbon carefully, determined to get it right this time.

This isn't my first stint helping Greta with a project, but I'm beginning to regret offering my aid on this one.

Damn, stupid ribbon.

When I started volunteering at the Suitor's Crossing Senior Center a few months ago, Greta and I immediately bonded over a mutual love for *Designing Women* reruns—a random fact we discovered while an episode aired during my first visit to the center.

"Trust me, no one will notice the ribbon. Bidders only care about the food." She folds the form in half then tucks it into the otherwise finished picnic basket in preparation for the auction in an hour.

It hearkens back to the town's early days. An old-fashioned way of dating when a man would guess his sweetheart's basket by its contents then bid to win a picnic with her.

Greta already has a beau, but that doesn't mean her basket can be a slouch, which is why she asked me to assemble it with all of his favorite items since her arthritis has been flaring up.

"Okay, how's that?" I tie off my last-ditch effort at a bow, and Greta smiles.

"It looks great. He's not going to know what hit him when he gets that basket."

"Well, I think he's going to have an idea," I tease, carrying the finished basket to the side table by the door. A glimpse at my reflection in the wall mirror has a grimace pulling at my mouth.

Tendrils of hair have fallen from my braid and glitter shimmers on my cheeks like a middle school girl heading to her first dance. I must have touched my face after messing with that damn ribbon. It only has hints of sparkle, but apparently, it's enough to leave traces wherever it lands.

Ignoring the glitter for now, I tug the band from the end of my braid to redo my hair into a semblance of pretty and respectable.

Greta may not think things need to be perfect, but there's more than impressing Mr. Caldwell at stake.

I'm also hoping to impress his grandson.

Not that he'll know you made the basket, or will notice your hair, or is aware that you even exist.

Griffen and I see each other around the senior center when he accompanies his grandfather, but we've never really spoken. The quiet giant likes to keep to himself, unless he's surrounded by his grandpa and his friends.

Sometimes one of the Caldwell siblings will visit, but for the most part, Griffen sticks to himself.

An attractive recluse I'd like to know better.

Maybe one of these days you'll gain the confidence to strike up a conversation.

Finishing the braid, I double-check every stray hair is in place then smile. Until then, I'll stick to the sidelines—looking as presentable as possible—in the hopes he'll notice me.

CHAPTER THREE

GRIFFEN

People clap as a red basket filled with Italian subs and homemade potato salad is won by Mr. Kaye. He shuffles as fast as he can with a cane to the front of the room to claim his prize, then the center's activity manager grabs another basket to auction.

Terrance reads from the piece of paper tucked in the basket. "We've got a Caesar salad, vanilla cake pops, and..."

Sighing, my gaze roams around the packed room. I hadn't planned on lingering for so long, since after Gramps wins Greta's basket, they'll immediately go enjoy the lunch she packed for him, and they don't need a third wheel on their date

But Gramps insisted I stay, and I couldn't tell the old man *no*, especially when our time sharing these kinds of events is limited.

Sure, I'm still going to see my grandpa regularly after he moves in with Greta, but it won't be the same. Not like when I drive him to the senior center and around town on errands. Not when the retirement community has its own mode of transportation for residents.

"Next up, we have this pretty blue and white gingham basket filled with bacon ranch pasta salad, salami pinwheels, and lemon crinkle cookies. Mmm, this is a good one, folks," Terrance calls out.

Ironically, those are some of *my* favorite picnic foods all in one basket as if it were made just for me.

"That one is Greta's," Gramps leans over to whisper.

Ah, that makes more sense.

Gramps and I share similar tastes, although he usually prefers iced oatmeal cookies over lemon.

"Let's start the bidding at $10."

I expect Grandpa's hand to go up immediately, but it remains in his lap. His gnarled knuckles flex, stretching the age-spotted skin.

"I thought you said that was Greta's basket."

"It is, but—" Gramps rubs his arm "—I'm feeling a little weak today. Do you mind bidding for me?"

A higher bid price is called out, and I raise my hand, concern etching my brow.

"Are you sure you're okay? If you're too weak to raise your arm, maybe we should see the doctor." Already, my phone is in hand, prepared to text my siblings to let them know I'm taking Gramps to the local urgent care.

"No, no... It's not serious enough for that." He bumps his knee against mine to halt my frantic typing. "I'll be fine. Just make sure you get my Greta's basket."

"Do I hear $50?"

I lift my hand again, torn between being safe and trusting Gramps's assessment. "If you start to feel worse, let me know. Greta will understand if you can't do the picnic today."

His chin dips in assent, urgency beaming from his eyes. "Alright, alright. Just don't let Geyser win."

Shaking my head at his stubbornness, my hand goes up again as a bidding war begins between me and Mr. Geyser. The old coot has been forcing higher bids all afternoon, though his aim isn't to claim a basket, he wants to earn as much money for the center as possible.

The proceeds from the auction will go toward a new shuffleboard for the senior center, and it's no secret how badly he wants one. Everyone has heard his tales of being a shuffleboard champion.

"$100 for this lovely basket. Do I hear $105? Going once..." Terrance looks around. "Going twice... Sold to Mr. Griffen Caldwell. Congratulations!"

The crowd cheers, and I sink lower in my seat, abhorring being the center of attention.

When the last basket is auctioned off, those who didn't win a basket head to the large cafeteria where a local church is providing a consolation lunch. Winners are asked to pay their bids to a woman seated up front.

Gramps hops to his feet with more energy than I would expect from a man purportedly too weak to bid on his own girlfriend's picnic basket. "Go find out where Greta's going to be, would ya? Let her know I'm going to be a little late."

"You are?" I ask, stretching my arms overhead. Sitting for an hour in a tiny metal chair not meant to hold someone my size has all my muscles cramping.

"Gotta stop by the can." Gramps pats his stomach before gesturing towards the bathroom.

I'd rather not dwell on why he thinks he's going to be in there for so long that he can't meet Greta in a timely manner, so I head to the lady collecting everyone's money for the baskets. Forking over a hundred dollars before she tells me where to meet Greta, who's setting up the picnic beside an oak tree outside.

Except when I near the spot, it's not an older woman with pink hair waiting for me. It's a much younger, *and curvier*, one—Heidi, the senior center's newest volunteer.

The woman Beckett teased me about.

The one he said is interested in me.

"Hey," I say awkwardly. My steps slow once the gold- and red-leaved branches overhead provide some shade. "This is Greta's basket, right?"

"Yeah, she wanted me to set it up because of her bad knees. It's tough for her to get up and down on the ground." Heidi lowers a navy blanket and pats the corners down before removing containers of food from a basket resting against the tree.

My brow wrinkles in confusion as I process her explanation.

"Seems like an odd place to choose for a picnic. The dirt is hardpacked and knotted with tree roots."

Heidi looks around. An adorable pucker pulls to the center of her forehead, and my fingers twitch to smooth the wrinkle.

"You know what? You're right. There are plenty of picnic tables she could have chosen instead of the grass. That's odd, right?"

Suspicion seeps into my gut. *Grandpa, no,* I moan internally.

"Did Greta say how long she'd be?"

"Nope, just that she would be a little late because she had to go to the bathroom."

This time I moan out loud.

"What's wrong?" Her gaze sweeps behind me, realizing someone else is missing from this equation. "Where's your grandpa?"

"Probably laughing his ass off with Greta because this is a setup. My grandpa gave the same bathroom excuse." And now it makes sense why it's my favorite food in that basket rather than his.

Her blue eyes widen in shock. "A setup? Between us?"

If I already didn't believe Beckett when he said Heidi was interested in me, her pure astonishment at the thought of us being on a date would have quickly snuffed out the idea.

She's not excited or eager.

She's shocked and unsure.

What the hell have you done, Gramps?

CHAPTER FOUR

HEIDI

Humiliation floods my system. *I'm going to kill Greta.* She's teased me about staring at Griffen—no matter how hard I try to not let my eyes drift his way—but to work together with his grandfather for this little ruse is beyond embarrassing.

Staring down at the blanket covered with Tupperware dishes full of what I'm guessing are *Griffen's* favorite foods, a sense of panic sets in.

My teeth nibble my lower lip as I contemplate our options. Follow through with the impromptu date, or part ways with a basket of too much food for one person?

"What should we do?" I ask.

Griffen's amber gaze bounces between me and the spread before us.

He clears his throat then gestures toward the food. His shaggy hair flops forward with the motion, tempting me to brush it back and test the softness. "No reason this should go to waste. Their plan might have been ridiculous, but no harm, no foul, right? I don't mind sharing lunch, if you don't."

"No, of course not! I'm Heidi, by the way." I hold my hand out to shake, and he gingerly takes it. The warmth of his palm engulfs mine, although he barely holds it before dropping it like a hot potato.

I scrub at the thigh of my jeans to dispel the lingering sparks from his touch, and he hones in on the movement, stern lines forming around his mouth.

Fuck... It probably looks like I think he has cooties or something.

Before I can come up with a reasonable excuse for the action—anything that paints me in a better light, but also keeps the secret of his effect on me—Griffen grunts his name, and I force a smile of acknowledgement.

It's not like I can admit to already knowing who he is. There's only so much embarrassment my self-esteem can handle in one day.

"Please sit. Enjoy!" I lower to the ground, tucking my legs beneath my butt. If I'd known Greta was going to trick me into a picnic date, I would have worn something more comfortable than jeans. The durable fabric cuts into my stomach and knees, and I pray my oversized sweater covers most of the awkward bulging.

Griffen slowly follows my lead and bends his large frame into a small enough ball to kind of fit on the blanket. Most of his body rests on sparse patches of grass and dirt—his attempt to not manspread and hog the entire area.

Not that I would mind being squished close to him.

He reminds me of a big teddy bear.

He has the typical gruff mountain man look, but I've seen the way he acts around his grandfather and the other seniors at the center. Griffen is as kind and gentle as can be.

So, cozied up to his protective warmth on a perfect fall day?

I wouldn't mind one damn bit.

Griffen pops a salami pinwheel in his mouth and chews before clearing his throat. "What made you decide to volunteer at the center?"

Grabbing my own pinwheel, I pick at the edge of the tortilla, thinking about the past and bittersweet memories.

"My grandparents were my favorite people growing up. I've felt each of their losses keenly, but it wasn't until the last one passed that grief really hit me." We lost her right before her eighty-seventh birthday a few months ago, and a familiar ache throbs in my chest as I remember the call from my mom, the funeral, going through Grandma Joyce's things to decide what to keep, donate, or sell.

"I guess I was searching for connection again, so when I saw the senior center was looking for more volunteers, I figured it was meant to be. Not everyone feels comfortable hanging out with older adults, but that's never been an issue for me."

Griffen nods in understanding. "Sorry about your grandparents."

"Thank you. They definitely left an impression on me."

"Do your parents live in town?"

I shake my head and stab a fork into a serving of the bacon ranch pasta salad. The creamy dressing and crunchy bacon bits combine into an explosion of flavor on my tongue, and a quiet hum of appreciation vibrates in my throat.

"No, they live in Guardian Valley, Montana. My maternal grandparents used to live here, though. They actually left me their house, which is why I moved to Suitor's Crossing."

For the first time, it occurs to me that they may not have been strangers to Griffen, a town local. "Maybe you knew them. The Schmidts?"

He thinks for a moment, staring up at the sky through branches of autumn leaves, then dips his chin down. "Sorry, the name doesn't ring a bell, but Gramps would probably recognize it. He's been around a lot longer than me."

"We should ask him some time. You're his caretaker, right? Do you enjoy it?" I question, already ninety-nine percent sure of the answer.

"For now." He shrugs his broad shoulders and relaxes against the massive tree trunk behind us. I consciously ignore the play of muscles beneath his flannel shirt with each shift. "He's moving in with Greta before Thanksgiving."

I mentally slap myself on the forehead. "I forgot she mentioned it the other day. How do you feel about the news?"

"I'm happy for them. Just have to figure out what to do with myself now that I don't have him to take care of. I do odd jobs at Hearthstone Lodge, but that's more of a part-time gig."

"And you're not interested in making it a full-time deal," I venture.

"I don't know. I've never really had a clear passion for one thing like my siblings. Beckett wanted to be a firefighter. Ezra wanted to go into business. Kennedy loves being creative and organizing, so they all found their niche. When it was decided that Gramps needed somebody to stay with him full-time—to keep an eye on him—the role naturally fell to me. I wasn't mad about it. It gave me an excuse not to dwell on not having a clue what to do with myself."

"I get that."

His head turns towards me, and a flush of red burns my cheeks under the weight of his attention. "What do you do?"

"Right now, I work at Design Time. In retail, not the embroidery stuff in the back of the store." Just the thought makes me shudder. I've seen how those employees are treated by my boss, especially since he lost an all-star embroiderer—*Avery something?*—a while back.

"I graduated in May with a fine arts degree that focused on photography, which probably wasn't the smartest decision, but it's my passion." I laugh. "Goes to show that even if you know what you want to do, it doesn't always mean you get to do it."

Griffen and I share a look of commiseration before he asks, "What kind of photography?"

"Mostly nature. Landscapes. I thought about asking Kent Moreland if I could intern or be an assistant, since he used to be a photojournalist in another life, but now that he's transitioned to people and events, I'm not sure he'd go for it."

"I bet he's still taking those types of photos, though, even if they're not for a job. It couldn't hurt to ask."

"You've got a point. Maybe I should reach out to him." It's not like all of his knowledge has dried up. I make a mental note to draft an email to send about potentially learning from him.

The conversation shifts to other topics as we eat.

There's a brief moment of self-consciousness after Griffen remarks on the glitter on my cheeks, and I realize I didn't scrub all the evidence of my fight with that ribbon away, but overall, we're strangely comfortable together.

Griffen is the perfect gentleman, and despite the introverted nature I observed in the past, he's easy to talk to. Not too many silences to make things awkward.

"Maybe we should thank Greta and your grandpa for their meddling," I tease as we pack up the empty food containers. "Lunch was fun."

"It was good... Do you need any help carrying that inside?" He points to the much lighter basket in my hand.

"Nah, I've got it. Thanks, though."

We stand there waiting for the other to say something more, but rather than ask for my number or suggest seeing each other again, Griffen steps back with a sigh.

"Guess I'll see you around. Thanks again for lunch." He offers a stiff wave then spins on his heel and hurries back to the senior center.

"Yeah, see you around," I say softly to his broad back as he walks away.

Guess it was too much to hope that a little matchmaking might actually work.

So much for Suitor's Crossing heart sparks.

CHAPTER FIVE

GRIFFEN

G ramps is nowhere to be found after my picnic with Heidi.
Probably off with Greta giggling over their little scheme.

I text to let him know I'm leaving, figuring Greta will give him a ride home, then drive out to the lodge. The aftermath of my afternoon with Heidi tingles in my veins, heightening the need for something to do with my hands.

The urge to release this pent-up energy.

"Why did you have to interfere, Gramps?" I groan to myself, scrubbing a hand down my bearded cheek.

Before the picnic, Heidi was a fantasy. A pretty daydream while I hung out at the senior center.

Now, she's real. I know how easy she is to talk to and how much I'd like to spend more time with her.

But that's a recipe for disaster.

We can't be more than friends, and *more* is exactly what I'm craving after one afternoon together.

"Fuck," I mutter.

The first and only time I tried to have sex, the girl laughed and called me a 'freak' because I was so big. Prom night is supposed to be momentous. Losing your virginity is practically a rite of passage.

Instead, it scarred me for life.

Because I never want to experience anything like that again.

I don't want to shock or hurt any woman, least of all Heidi. And I definitely don't want to be humiliated and reminded that there's something wrong with me.

Which means today's picnic is all we'll ever have.

Hearthstone Lodge's automatic doors swoosh open with a waft of autumn spices in the air. The lobby is decorated with apples, pumpkins, and haybales, thanks to my sister Kennedy, and the huge fireplace off to the side is lit with cheerful flames in front of several occupied leather couches.

My older brother Ezra rounds the concierge desk with a grin. "Hey, Griff, how's it going? I heard about your date today." He slaps my back in greeting before guiding me to the rear of the lobby where windows provide a gorgeous view of the mountains.

"News travels fast in this family," I grunt.

"We can't help ourselves, especially when it comes to our little brother's happiness. How was it? Beckett said the girl really likes you."

"Beckett needs to mind his own business." My booted footsteps pick up speed as I stomp through French doors leading to the back terraces.

"Oh, so you really like her, too."

"Who does Griff like?" Kennedy joins our group, and I roll my eyes heavenward.

How many more of my siblings are hiding out in the lodge today?

I should have gone to the stables. Soren wouldn't hound me about this kind of stuff.

Maybe.

Probably.

"Heidi, his picnic date," Ezra explains as he wraps an arm around Kennedy's shoulders and squeezes her into his side for a quick hug.

"Oh, the woman Gramps and Greta set you up with? I heard she's really sweet."

"She is." No use lying. Heidi is sweet and pretty and not meant for me.

"When are you going to see her again?"

"Guess whenever I go to the senior center." My shoulders rise and fall in feigned nonchalance. Like it doesn't matter to me if our paths cross again or not. Like I'm not already hooked on her cozy vanilla scent or the temptation of those generous curves she tried to hide under a large sweater.

"I was talking about a date." Kennedy pokes my ribs. "Did you get her number?"

"Nope."

"Why not? It didn't go well?"

"It went fine. Can we stop with the twenty questions?" There's a slight growl to my voice, and I swallow the primal sound before it grows louder in frustration.

"Geez, Griff, what's gotten into you? I know what Gramps did was a surprise, but it wasn't mean-spirited. No need to be angry about it."

"I'm not angry."

"Right."

Now both my siblings sport matching scowls.

"I want to be alone, okay?" I burst out of the dense foliage of a trail that leads toward the stables. Ezra and Kennedy stop, silently giving me what I want, but I know this conversation isn't over.

Hopefully, Soren isn't available to continue the interrogation.

All I want is to toss hay, muck stalls, and get one curvy girl out of my head.

Is that too much to ask?

CHAPTER SIX

HEIDI

It's a week before I see Griffen again.

He's sitting at a table with three other women, helping one knit a scarf by holding a ball of yarn for her. It's freaking adorable, and I would love to snap a picture, but I don't think that would go over too well.

"You're staring again. Why don't you go over and talk to him?" Greta bumps my shoulder with hers.

"That's enough from you," I scold. "You did your part, and now it's up to him."

"It's the twenty-first century. You don't have to wait for the man to come to you. Look at how I got Don. You think I was waiting around for him to approach me?" An amused cackle rocks her slim form. "Hardly. Men need a push."

"And that man?" She points to Griffen as if he can't see her gesturing to him from across the room. "Needs more of a push than others. Griffen's always been a sweetheart, but he's also shy. He needs a little help, and that's where you come in."

"That is *not* where I come in," I retort.

Even if I were brave enough to approach Griffen, I'm not sure what I'd say. No way my courage extends to asking him out on a date.

As if sensing we're talking about him, Griffen looks up from the knitting and catches my eye. I smile and wave, but he quickly ducks his head with a frown, pretending he didn't see me.

Ouch.

Thankfully, Greta didn't catch the exchange. I'd hate to know what she would do then.

Actually, I hate what my body is starting to do *now* as tears well in my eyes.

"Um, didn't you say you forgot your glasses back in the sewing room? Let me grab those for you."

"Oh, you don't..."

I'm gone before Greta can finish her protest. I need a minute alone, and the empty sewing room, which is closed at this time of day, is the perfect escape.

The door closes with a click behind me, and I sigh in relief as tears fall down my cheeks. I can't believe he ignored me like that.

Just pretended that I didn't exist.

It's not like I expect him to declare his undying love for me. A brief acknowledgement, a *hello*, wouldn't give me the wrong impression, but apparently, even that is too much for him.

A shuddery breath rattles from my lungs. Sniffling, I swipe at the tears, annoyed with myself.

"I shouldn't be crying over a man," I say out loud, as if that'll make a difference—reprimanding myself for my own feelings.

The sound of the door opening and closing echoes in the room. Spinning around, my watery gaze meets Griffen's.

"What are you doing here?"

Why did he follow me? Isn't it enough that he ignored me? Now he wants to catch me crying over his rejection?

"I came to apologize." The toe of his boot scuffs at the floor as he runs a hand through his wavy hair.

"For what?"

"For being an ass out there. I don't know what I was think—"

"I can tell you what you were thinking," I interrupt, pain in my voice. "There's that girl I was forced to have a fake date with. The one I was hoping to never see again."

Maybe that's dramatic, but I'm *feeling* dramatic after the past ten minutes.

"What? No. I loved our date. Our *real* date," he emphasizes. "But it can't go anywhere. I can't date anyone."

"What? Why? Do you already have a girlfriend?"

"No."

"A boyfriend?" Maybe that explains why Greta said she's never heard of him being romantically involved with a woman.

"No."

"You've secretly become a monk and taken a vow of celibacy?"

Griffen chuckles and leans against the wall, resting his head against the exposed brick. "Nope, although that sounds less humiliating than the truth."

"Try me," I say, crossing my arms over my chest, intensely curious about his reasons.

"You may have noticed that I'm big." He gestures to his large stature, and my eyes take the opportunity to scan his body appreciatively.

"Yeah," I say slowly. What's his size have to do with anything?

Honestly, it should be a plus.

Who doesn't want a tall, bear-like man who can wrap you in his burly arms to keep you warm at night?

I know I sure as hell do.

He swallows hard, his Adam's apple bobbing in his throat.

"Well, at my high school prom," he says derisively, "Susie Baker and I decided we'd lose our virginities to each other."

Not where I was expecting this to go, but okay.

"Except we didn't get that far. She started laughing after she saw my dick. Called me a 'freak.' Alluded to my size being the problem. I vowed from then on that I would never try again. I don't want to hurt anyone, and I don't want to be ridiculed. My body isn't made for that kind of intimacy."

"Bullshit."

"Excuse me?"

Maybe I shouldn't have said that out loud, but come on, I've read the books. Seen some quality erotic films.

I know it can work.

"You're not too big, Griffen. You were inexperienced, and so was Susie. The first time can be scary for a lot of girls, and if you are proportionate…" My gaze drops down to his groin. "Like I assume you are, then it makes sense that she overreacted. That doesn't excuse her cruelty, though, or mean you should give up forever. You're not a freak. You deserve love and happiness."

"Heidi, I appreciate what you are—"

"Stop." I step closer, put my hands on his shoulders for leverage, then haul myself to my tiptoes. "You're not a freak," I repeat in a whisper, then slam my mouth over his, stealing the protest from his lips.

Griffen can argue all he wants, but he's not going to dissuade me.

If what's stopping him from giving me a chance is fear, not disinterest, then I am perfectly fine proving there's nothing wrong, or *freakish*, about him.

It seems I'm the one with a bit of experience in this arena, and it gives me just enough courage to take what I want.

First?

A kiss from my sweet, but clueless mountain man.

CHAPTER SEVEN

GRIFFEN

My entire body freezes beneath Heidi. After explaining why things couldn't go any further between us, I wasn't expecting her to kiss me.

Instinctively, my hands go to her wide hips and squeeze, torn between pushing her away for her own good and pulling her closer for mine.

Shouldn't she be hesitant?

Worried about my size?

"Stop thinking," she murmurs. "Trust me to know what I can handle."

Heidi retreats long enough to look up into my eyes. Sincerity rings clear in hers, and for the first time, I wonder if maybe I haven't been overzealous in how much I've avoided women and relationships.

If Heidi is willing to take a chance on me, then maybe I've been wrong all these years.

"Trust me... Kiss me..."

It's hard for me to ignore her plea, so I tentatively brush my lips over hers.

It's careful.

Soft.

Gentle caresses exploring each other's boundaries until our desire escalates, and we end up against a counter, Heidi pinned between my arms, her lush body arching into mine with reckless abandon.

One of her legs wraps around my waist as she grinds her pussy along the hard ridge of my dick.

"Fuck," I whisper. I haven't done anything like this in over a decade, and even then, it was nowhere near as explosive.

"We can't do that yet," she taunts. "Not here."

Though that doesn't stop her from continuing the rhythm of rocking and rubbing.

Her breasts press into my chest, lifting the pale flesh into an obscene display above her shirt's neckline, and my tongue aches to trace the delicate veins leading to her nipples.

I'm not ready to completely abandon my fears about being too big for her. But where's the harm in a little touching and dry humping?

Lifting Heidi onto the counter to better suit our heights, my covered cock shunts between the seam of her jeans, and we both moan.

"Griffen, more…"

I want to please her, but I'm as close to a virgin as a man can get.

That doesn't stop me from trying, though.

My palms slide under her shirt, skimming the softness of her belly before cupping her breasts. They fill my large palms just right—so right that I have to see.

Lifting the fabric higher so it bunches under her arms, I lick my lips at the sight of her pinkened tits supported by a nude bra.

I gently fold the cups underneath her trembling flesh to reveal the engorged nipples.

"You're so pretty," I rasp in awe.

"You can kiss them if you want."

I can't refuse her invitation.

So, I bend down to suck one of the nipples into my mouth, licking at the berry tip as my teeth graze the sensitive skin.

Heidi arches into my embrace, whimpering at the onslaught of sensations. My cock grinding into her clit. My lips suckling at her sweet tits.

She's close.

I feel it.

The primal instinct when a man is pleasuring his woman.

But she's not willing to go off alone. Her fingers inch beneath my flannel and scratch at my chest and stomach.

The sharp pain heightens my pleasure. Drives me into a frenzy of practically fucking her into the linoleum counter top.

Until we both cry out with our orgasms.

Shaking, sweating, gasping for a reality that disappeared the moment Heidi kissed me.

"Wow," she says, slumping into my arms, her cheek resting where my heart pounds in my chest.

"Yeah, wow," I agree.

Maybe learning what I've been missing all these years should suck, but I don't regret my past decisions.

A random hookup with someone else wouldn't have been anywhere near as satisfying as being with Heidi.

"You're okay?" Despite keeping our clothes on, I need her reassurance.

"I'm perfect. So are you." She smiles, then presses a gentle kiss to my lips. "Told you there wasn't anything to be afraid of."

I help straighten out her clothes then lower her back to the ground.

Not addressing her comment.

Because what can I say?

I'm still worried about my size and don't want to hurt Heidi.

I don't want her to turn away from me in disgust either.

CHAPTER EIGHT

HEIDI

Greta's knowing gaze examines my messed-up hair and wrinkled clothes. My lips are probably swollen and reddened, too.

"Hmm..." Greta drawls. "Somebody enjoyed the sewing room. I see you forgot my glasses as well."

She winks, and I check my hands as if surprised.

"Um, yeah. I couldn't find them," I lie.

"Probably because you were too busy with your shenanigans with Griffen."

"Greta."

"No need to be embarrassed. It's natural for two young people to let their passions rule. I'm happy that you and Griffen have come to an understanding."

"I don't know what you're talking about," I snip.

A couple of other seniors stare at me then Griffen, sly smiles on their faces. Clearly, it's no secret what we were doing in that room for so long.

Perhaps I should be more ashamed that the entire senior center seems to know that Griffen and I were making out and grinding like a couple of teens.

But I don't care.

It was too glorious to feel shame.

And, hopefully, this is just the beginning of something more.

FALLEN LEAVES CRUNCHES beneath my car tires as I park in front of Kent Moreland's house.

After several emails back and forth, he agreed to meet with me to discuss becoming his assistant—a step up from the unpaid intern position I was imagining.

Kent steps onto his porch and waves while I grab my portfolio from the backseat.

"You must be Heidi," he says, offering his hand to shake in greeting.

"Guilty. Thank you for responding to my email. I'm sure you get a lot of spam requests to work together for a fee," I joke.

Sometimes, Mike at Design Time has me post to the store's social media feeds, and even his small-town operation fields messages from bots and scammers.

A warm chuckle transforms Kent's austere features into a friendly welcome as he waves me inside. "I get my fair share, but it's usually pretty easy to tell who's real and who's fake. My office is down the hall, so we can chat more there."

A gray cat accompanies our trek to his office, and I bend to brush a quick pet over its head before it races ahead to weave between Kent's feet.

Straightening, I glance over the walls. For a photographer, there aren't many photos hung up. The decor is mostly wood or metal art pieces and colorful items that speak of his travels around the world.

Strange... or maybe he's modest.

"Have a seat. I can take a look at your portfolio while you share what your goals are if I hire you as my assistant."

An imaginary flag drops before me, signaling the start of what could be the job that launches my career into photography. Despite Kent's isolation in Suitor's Crossing, people still know his name. He's a renowned photojournalist, even if he is retired.

I launch into my credentials and plans for the future. It's been a while since I've had to sell myself and my photography skills. My retail position at Design Time didn't require much more from me than assuring Mike I could work certain shifts.

To be honest, if that interview hadn't worked out, I would have applied somewhere else, no big deal.

But this is a chance to work with Kent Moreland.

In his email response, he'd told me how he'd been considering hiring an assistant, and it felt like fate the moment I read those words.

And isn't Suitor's Crossing all about the magic of fate? I mean technically that applies to love and soulmates, or *heart sparks*, but in a roundabout way, this is still kind of connected.

Being set up with Griffen pushed me to reach out to Kent. Our conversation made me think about what I want from my life—a career to enjoy and a man to love.

I already have a head start in the love department, thanks to Greta and Mr. Caldwell's interference, which just leaves my professional life.

If you were brave enough to kiss Griffen first, then you are definitely badass enough to ace this interview.

Meeting Kent's kind eyes, I toss him a winning smile.

Hell, yeah, I've got this.

CHAPTER NINE

GRIFFEN

Heidi's name pops up on my phone screen while I finish fixing a loose leg on one of the terrace chairs at the lodge.

I've spent the morning and afternoon systematically working down the list Soren left for me in the tiny office I have at Hearthstone.

The private space was a nice gesture by Ezra, but as a part-time employee whose job requires me to be on the move, an office outfitted with a desk and computer weren't really necessary.

I swipe my thumb across the screen to answer Heidi's call.

"Hey, what's up?"

"I got the job!" Her excited squeal pierces through the speaker. "I'm officially Kent Moreland's assistant. Well, sort of. I have to give Mike my two weeks' notice, but then I'm free to accompany Kent on his gigs."

"Congratulations! How should we celebrate?" I tuck the phone between my ear and shoulder as I scrub my hands free of dirt with a rag from my toolbox.

"Dinner at The Ole Aces?"

"Sounds good. Does six work for you? I've got a couple more things to do at the lodge, then I'll need to shower. After that, I can pick you up."

"I'll be waiting. See you soon!"

THE OLE ACES USED TO be home to the grittier element of Suitor's Crossing, but once military veteran Austin Fielding bought it, he turned it into one of the best places to chill with friends and a beer.

There was a rowdy transition period—especially after his Reaper's Wolves MC friends became regular patrons—but with the completion of renovations, the bar hasn't seen a major brawl in a while.

Heidi and I shuffle into a booth with wooden privacy slats rising from the back of our seats. The rustic grain gleams under the warm glow of the industrial lamps installed overhead, and my fingers itch to explore the craftsmanship.

"Is there a spider or something up there?" Heidi asks, tilting her head upward to search for what's captured my attention.

"Ah, no... Just admiring Rhys's work."

Unfamiliarity wrinkles her brow.

"Rhys is a local blacksmith." I point to the metal pieces mounted around the bar. "He created all of the iron fixtures and the barstool bases."

"Oh, wow." Heidi looks around the room with new eyes.

Her expression grows in appreciation as she studies each design, and a nudge in my gut whispers that I should tell her the whole truth.

"I see the appeal. They're really cool—modern yet still blending seamlessly with the rusticity of the wood."

A waitress stops by to take our drink order, saving me from immediately admitting the true reason for my fascination. Something I haven't shared with anyone, not even my family.

Scratching behind my ear, I swallow the lump of nerves lodged in my throat. "Actually, it's more than admiration. I'm interested in learning about smithing. There was a one-off project I did in my high school woodshop class—a simple metal shelf—and since then, I've thought about exploring more."

"So, you *do* know what you'd like to pursue once your grandpa moves to Golden Living."

I flush in remembrance of telling her that I didn't have a clue what my life should look like after Gramps's move. I wasn't intentionally lying to her, but maybe I'd been lying to myself. Doubting the seriousness of my interest. Ignoring the instinct to make the dream a reality.

"I guess so. Maybe..." I shrug in discomfort. "No one in my family knows. It's just been an idea in the back of my head for years. Hearing you talk about studying under Kent, then chasing your dream to make it happen, really inspired me. Maybe I should approach Rhys about an apprenticeship."

Encouragement beams from her warm gaze. "You should! Even if his answer is *no*, he could offer suggestions for other blacksmiths to contact."

Heidi reaches across the table to squeeze my tight fist. My knuckles are white from the pressure, but her supportive touch eases some of the tension.

"You don't think I'm too old to be an apprentice? I'm thirty years old and still don't know what I want to be when I grow up," I joke.

"Thirty is not old." She rolls her eyes. "And tons of people don't have their lives figured out at every age. The important thing is to never give up or settle for less than you deserve. Maybe you start apprenticing and find out it's not for you, but at least you'll know, and you'll be free to explore another interest. It won't be hanging over your head as a *'what if'* that stops you from pursuing anything else for decades."

I turn my hand over to tangle my fingers with hers. "You're pretty smart, you know that?"

"I do, but it never hurts to hear it again." A mischievous grin breaks through the intensity of her pep talk. "Whatever you decide, I'm here for you."

Raising her hand to my lips, I press a kiss to the delicate skin and exhale the riot of nerves our conversation brought up.

It's good to know I'm not being unrealistic or ridiculous. My siblings would have told me the same thing, but having Heidi fully support my secret dream is an entirely different feeling.

Like anything is possible as long as she's by my side.

CHAPTER TEN

HEIDI

A rush of autumn air flits through the crack of the passenger's side window. It's a little too cool to roll it all the way down, but I don't mind. The combination of heat blowing from the vents of Griffen's truck and the brisk chill from outside creates the perfect cozy cocoon.

"Want to wander the trails behind Hearthstone, or are you ready to go home?" Griffen asks, his right hand covering mine on the console.

"A walk sounds nice, especially with the full moon tonight."

He nods then turns onto another road that will lead us to his family's lodge. The drive isn't long, and soon we're ambling down a worn dirt path that circles a pond reflecting the moon and trees.

"Do you think you'll still work at the lodge if Rhys takes you on as an apprentice?" My question interrupts the comfortable symphony of leaves crackling beneath our boots and the rustling of critters settling in for the evening.

Broad shoulders rise and fall in nonchalance. "Probably. Hearthstone will always be part of my family's legacy. Once I have enough experience, maybe I can contribute more than my handyman skills. Ezra already sources whatever the lodge needs locally, so I don't foresee him having an issue letting me provide a decorative light fixture or table set here and there."

"I haven't met your brother, but I'm sure you're right."

"We need to rectify that, you know. All of my siblings want to meet you."

"Really?" Nerves tangle in my belly. I've heard stories about the Caldwell brood from Greta, Gramps, and Griffen—not to mention, they're sort of unavoidable in Suitor's Crossing as one of the town's founding families. They're basically local royalty.

Which adds to the pressure of meeting Griffen's family as his... girlfriend? *Heart spark*? We haven't labeled the fragile bond between us yet.

"Yep... Technically, you've been invited to the past two Sunday family dinners, but selfishly, I've wanted to keep you to myself," he says sheepishly. My hand tightens around his where it swings by our hips. "You're aware of my hangups with sex and relationships, but they're not. All they know is that I'm a bit of a recluse when it comes to women."

"A bit?" I tease, leaning into his side.

A bark of self-deprecating laughter rumbles from his chest. "Okay, a lot. But what we're doing, it's new territory for me. I'm trying to recalibrate my thinking... while also just being plain possessive." He shoots a sly grin my way. "My siblings can be overwhelming. They'll want to hog all of your attention, and I'm not ready for that."

"I understand." And I do, although a part of me wishes he felt differently. "Speaking of recalibrating your thinking..."

We're far enough away from the lodge that the glow of lights surrounding it barely penetrates the woods around us, which has a wholly inappropriate idea taking root.

Twisting in front of Griffen, my hands land on his chest and deliberately push him until his back braces against the bark of a large tree, shadows sliding forward to hide us from prying eyes.

"What if we work on showing you that there's nothing to worry about when it comes to your... *ahem*... package." My gaze drops to the length resting against his thigh.

"Heidi..."

I push to my tiptoes to steal whatever he was going to say—denial or agreement.

I've never been the aggressor with men, but it's empowering showing Griffen what could be. And he never takes long to adjust before snatching back control.

"Let me do this for you. For us," I murmur, pressing one more hard kiss to his lips before lowering to my knees on the cold forest floor.

His fingers wind through my loose hair to tug at the back until my eyes meet his. In the dark, only glimmers of lust and need are visible, but it's enough to tell me how he desires this just as much as me.

The sides of his unbuttoned flannel flap open as my nails scrape down his firm abdomen beneath a white tee. God, he's so burly—a mountain man meant just for me.

I fumble with the belt buckle and top button of his jeans, too distracted by my good fortune, but finally, I have what I want: Griffen's hard cock free from obstruction.

His grip in my hair flexes as I stare in awe.

If I were an eighteen-year-old virgin, the sight might intimidate me—although I'll never understand why that Susie girl had to be so cruel to Griffen—but I'm not a young girl.

I'm a fucking woman.

And Griffen's huge dick is taunting me with its thick girth, unreal length—*is that ten inches?*—and the gleam of fluid spilling from its broad head.

I've never been particularly fond of blowjobs.

Haven't given many.

But with Griffen?

I want to erase those bad memories and replace them with this: my touch, my reaction to his definitely *not* freakish dick.

"You're magnificent." The words are an exhalation of praise. A promise to appreciate him for everything he is.

"You don't have to say that. I know it's—Fuck! Heidi!"

Right, I'm *recalibrating his thinking*, which means no more insults from this man about his body.

Fucking Susie.

If I ever meet that woman, and let's face it, it's a small town, our running into each other is highly likely, I'll be sure to give her a piece of my mind.

I'm only able to fit about half of his cock in my mouth at first, vowing internally to practice slowly easing him down my throat like a fucking pro, but until then, I wrap a hand around his base, mouth and palm working in tandem.

"Goddamn, you look so pretty on your knees for me, baby."

That's more like it.

Dirty talk, not self-slander.

Moaning, I increase my efforts, determined to please Griffen. Saliva slicks down my chin as my jaw begins to ache, and an echoing ache throbs between my thighs.

"Fuck... I can't believe how well you're taking me," he rasps. "Your lips are stretched so wide. All I can imagine is how well your pussy will stretch for me. Maybe you *can* take me, huh, Heidi baby?"

Unable to nod in agreement, I suck hard at his tip instead, my tongue lapping at the gush of precum.

It's not long before he roars with satisfaction and jets of cum overflow my mouth. I try my damnedest to swallow most of his release, but the man's a giant—*giant dick, giant balls*—there's no way I can catch every last drop.

Once Griffen shudders a final time, I carefully let his cock slip free, tuck him back into his boxer briefs and jeans, then swipe the back of my hand over my mouth. Judging by the cool wetness on my chin, it doesn't do much.

"Here, let me." Griffen sheds his flannel and uses the hem to gently wipe away his cum and my spit.

I want to make a joke about him being a true gentleman, but I don't.

Because it's the truth.

Kind and tender. He makes me feel cared for. Seen. Respected.

And no other man could be better.

CHAPTER ELEVEN

GRIFFEN

It's Moving Day for Gramps, and all the Caldwells and their significant others are at the cabin hauling boxes out to trucks and preparing for the small trip to Golden Living.

These past few weeks have been a study in contrast.

A part of me has been sad as I've helped Gramps pack his clothes and mementos.

But another part has been exceedingly happy as Heidi and I continue to meet at the senior center. Going on dates around town to explore the charm of Suitor's Crossing. Making out and teasing each other with suggestive touches and continual grinding.

Our clothes never come completely off, but it's still been satisfying as hell.

"How are you doing, Griff?" Gramps pats my shoulder as the last of his boxes are dumped into my truck by Wyatt and Beckett.

"I'm good. How are you feeling? It's the end of an era."

"And the beginning of a new one full of love." A far-off look enters his eyes. "That's what I wanted to talk to you about."

"Okay..." My brow furrows. He's aware of me and Heidi; we haven't exactly been discreet. Plus, he and Greta can't resist teasing us over their trick at the picnic basket auction.

"I know what you and Miss Heidi have been up to at the center."

A blush rises to my cheeks.

"I've noticed a change in you; your siblings have, too. It's been great seeing you open up to somebody, and Heidi is a good girl. But I also know you've got some flawed thoughts about yourself in that hard head. Which is the only explanation I can think of for why Heidi isn't here today with the rest of your family."

I'm not sure how to respond.

Because he's right.

Heidi should be here, and I should stop holding back my feelings out of fear. Especially when she's already done a lot to convince me that those old concerns are baseless.

"Give her a chance. Your brothers and sister took risks, and you see how happy they are. That could be you and Heidi."

"Thanks, Gramps."

He's got me considering my brothers.

They *are* big. Soren is the closest in size to me, and I've never heard of problems with women. With any of my brothers.

Hell, Beckett fucked around all the time before falling for Beth.

Maybe I owe it to myself and Heidi to let go of the past.

I mean she's my fucking *heart spark*.

So, why the hell isn't she here?

After getting Gramps settled at Golden Living but promising to be back for a Sunday dinner of pizza and beer, I make a stop at an adult store on the outskirts of town before driving to Heidi's place.

If we're really about to take the next step in our relationship, then I'm going to do everything I can to ensure Heidi is ready to take *me*, including providing proper lubrication and something to stretch her before my cock gets anywhere near her pussy.

Her mouth sucks you just fine. Why would her pussy be any different?

I ignore the snip of logic as my fist knocks on her door, wondering what she'll think of my hastily made plan.

A minute later, the dark oak swings open to reveal a surprised Heidi in comfy leggings, tank top, and a long cardigan.

"Griffen, I wasn't expecting you today. How did moving go?"

"Fine. Can I come in?"

She jolts at my abruptness but waves me forward. "Sure."

Nerves clamber beneath my skin as I drag a steadying breath into my lungs and step into a cozy living room.

I learned during one of our conversations that most of the furniture is original to the house, collected by her grandparents over decades, so it's like stepping into a time capsule.

"Is something wrong? What's in your hand?" She gestures toward the bag I'm holding.

"Um... Everything's fine." A red flush burns the tips of my ears. *Here goes nothing.* "This is something for us, if you're interested."

I set the bag on a nearby table with a lace doily. The crinkle of plastic cuts through the awkward tension in the room.

"You know I've been afraid of our relationship progressing further because I don't want to hurt you. Or freak you out."

Heidi sighs. "Griffen, trust that I know—"

I lift my hands to stop her protests. She's been trying to convince me for weeks that I should trust her to know what she can handle.

I'm finally willing to listen and take that leap.

"I'm here because I don't want to do this halfway with you anymore. I want to be all in. I brought these things to help us."

I pull out a bottle of lube and a large dildo. When I checked out at the register, it'd been awkward as hell while the store employee punched in a code for the blue rubber phallus, but I'll do anything for Heidi.

Even stand embarrassed in front of a total stranger while they ring up sex toys.

"Oh, wow!" Heidi's brows raise to her hairline as she traces the label on the lube. "That's really sweet of you, and I'm curious to know what brought this on, but I have a confession to make."

She grabs my hand and leads me down the hall to her bedroom. Pastels decorate the walls and bedding.

Soft and pretty just like her.

She releases my hand long enough to reach under her bed and pull out a pink box. It lightly bounces on the mattress before Heidi taps the top lid and removes it.

"You see, I already have a treasure trove of toys and lube." She finds a half-empty bottle and shakes it. "We can use the stuff you brought, but I want to make it clear that I'm ready for you. I can take you. We don't need to wait any longer."

Damn, looks like my girl is still schooling me.

I study the variety of toys in her box before shaking my head in awe and pulling her in for a kiss. My tongue ravages hers as we stumble backward and fall onto the mattress.

Fearing I'm crushing her, I immediately roll to my side.

"Are you okay? I didn't hurt you, did I?"

"No, get back here." Heidi tugs on my shoulders to roll me back, and I follow her direction, kissing and nipping at her lips as she scratches at my neck and scalp.

"Too many clothes," she murmurs, and quickly we rip off our clothing until we're both naked on her bed.

The pink box tumbled on its side sometime during our mad dash to strip, so a variety of sex toys surrounds us, one digging uncomfortably into my hip.

"Griffen." Heidi's legs wrap around my waist, her wet folds cushioning my cock as it glides through her slick arousal.

"Not yet."

Even if Heidi thinks she's ready, I still need to ascertain that for myself.

I kiss down her chest, sucking on her nipples before going lower, licking her belly button and down her hip before burrowing between her thighs, carefully widening her legs for a prime view of her pussy.

"Holy fuck," I rasp, my mouth suddenly dry at the tempting sight. "I need to taste you first. Need you soft and accepting before giving you my cock, and an orgasm seems like the way to go."

"By all means," she laughs, allowing her knees to fall to the mattress.

Diving forward, I immediately lap from pussy hole to clit, before latching onto the bundle of nerves and sucking, as two fingers ease into her channel. I scissor them open to stretch her tight muscles and groan at the hot clasp around me.

If I manage to work my cock into this little pussy, it's going to feel damn good, but it still feels like a big *if*.

My beard grazes her inner thighs while my nose, mouth, and chin drown in her sweet juices.

Fuck, my girl is delicious.

Reluctantly removing my fingers from her cunt, I pat the bedding, searching for the perfect toy to send her over the edge. I may be a novice, but I'm no stranger to getting my woman off.

Not after the weeks we've spent together.

A glittery purple dildo bumps the back of my hand.

That'll do.

I drag the bulbous head through her sticky arousal, debating whether I should add more artificial lubrication, but Heidi's hand covers mine and urges the toy into her pussy.

"Don't make me wait, Griffen."

Trusting her, I shove the toy deeper while my head drops to play with her clit again.

"Such a sweet, dirty girl," I growl, reveling in the explicit sounds of a very wet cunt being licked and fucked. "You like fucking my face while I stuff this rubber dick inside your tight pussy?"

"Y-Yesss..." she mewls. Her hair spreads in a tangled mess on the pillow. The floral comforter scrunches beneath her tense fingers.

My girl is a gorgeous sight to behold. Full of lush curves that wiggle and wobble with each shuddering breath she takes.

Until a shout rises from her throat, and her release squirts into my mouth.

A sense of pride swells in my chest.

Heidi has been a lot of my firsts. She's the only woman I've ever given an orgasm to, the only one whose pussy I've devoured, and I'm addicted.

Hell, I've been addicted to Heidi for a while now.

"Come here," she orders, and I crawl back up her generous curves for another kiss. "I've got an idea on how to ease your fears. Do you trust me?"

"Always."

She grins, then points to the bed. "All right, mountain man, on your back."

I roll over, and Heidi whips her leg over my body to straddle my abdomen.

"This way, I can take you as deep as I want, and you don't have to worry about hurting me because I'm in control, okay?"

I nod.

She works her hips back until the tip of my cock finds the hot clutch of her cunt, then she slowly eases down the hard length, adjusting as she goes until she's fully seated on my thick cock.

"See? That wasn't so hard, was it?"

My teeth grind together as I focus on not blowing my load so soon. Her pussy is strangling my dick, clenching and pulsing in an erotic game. It's fucking amazing.

"This doesn't hurt you?" I grit out.

"No... It burns. A *good* burn," she confirms, before swiveling her hips and rubbing her clit against my pelvis.

A slow rhythm begins between us, then picks up speed. The sloppy sounds of sex ring in the air as Heidi gets wetter and wetter, soaking my cock in her juices.

"I'm not gonna last, baby," I grunt. My hand has never felt this good, and as much as I'd like to hold on, I'm worried I'll explode before she comes.

"Touch my clit."

Immediately, my thumb roughly circles the sensitive button.

Knowing how much she loves when I talk filthy, I growl, "Come on, baby. You wanted this monster cock buried in your cunt. You craved my fat dick, didn't you? Whispering, *trust me*. Begging me for it."

"Yes, Griffen... Yesss!" Heidi throws her head back with a scream, and I finally let go. Hot ropes of cum barrel free, overflowing between us to create a squishy mess, as a rain of sparks burn across my skin.

"Told you we would fit," Heidi says as she collapses on my chest.

"I should have trusted you all along."

"Now, you know for the future," she taunts, and I wrap my arms around her, grateful that we *have* a future.

I'm not a freak, maybe I never was.

And I'll forever be grateful to the beautiful woman warming my chest for showing me how wrong I was.

EPILOGUE

HEIDI

THREE YEARS LATER

B eing four months pregnant is no joke.
Heartburn, peeing all the time.

It definitely has its lows, but experiencing Griffen in full protective caretaker mode is sexy as hell.

"Do you need anything else, baby?" He opens a cool water bottle for me to guzzle.

"No, this is good, thank you."

He hovers at my side like he wants to say something else, so I wait patiently. Griffen likes to think before he speaks, which I appreciate. He's still a man of few words, but at least he's *my* man.

"I've been thinking..." he starts, "with the baby on the way, it might be nice to be near your parents. Our grandparents have had such an impact on our lives. Seems right that our own child has that same experience."

My brow wrinkles. "But my parents live in Montana," I remind him.

"I know," he nods. "I think we should split our time between Guardian Valley and Suitor's Crossing, so our kid gets the best of both worlds. Both of our families."

"You would do that for us?" Tears shimmer in my eyes, emotion overwhelming me.

Griffen's entire life is in Suitor's Crossing.

All of his siblings, nieces and nephews, Gramps and Greta. They're my family now, too, but I do miss my parents, aunts, uncles, and friends in Guardian Valley.

Plus, he finished his apprenticeship with Rhys two months ago. Isn't it too soon to leave his mentor?

"I would do anything for you. You should know that by now. Besides, I've talked with your dad, and there's a parcel of land for sale. It already has a house and some outbuildings. Maybe I can convert one into a forge."

"That would be perfect," I gush, impressed with how much he's thought this through.

The man has a serious plan, though that doesn't surprise me. Griffen is always putting family first and considering how best to care for us.

"It'll be perfect because we're together."

"Always." I smile, then kiss my husband.

My gentle mountain man, my *heart spark*.

Curious about Guardian Valley, Montana and the rugged heroes who call it home? Binge the complete *Heirs of Guardian Valley* series here[1]!

---

1. https://steamyromancereads.com/products/heirs-of-guardian-valley-series-e-book-bundle

THANKS FOR READING & DON'T FORGET TO RATE/ REVIEW!

Please consider leaving a rating/review. Ratings & reviews are the #1 way to support an indie author like me.

Also, don't miss out on free books and up-to-date release information. You can sign up for my newsletter here[1].

I appreciate your support!

XO, Hallie

---

1. https://www.thearrowedheart.com/hallie-bennett

ABOUT THE AUTHOR

Hallie prefers steamy, insta-love stories where curvy girls are claimed by filthy-talking heroes. And when she ran out of reading material, she decided to write her own stories. If you want a quick, hot read, she's your girl!